P9-EAO-950

I Love
Birthdays

For Ana Vivas, thank you

SIMON & SCHUSTER BOOKS FOR YOUNG READERS
An imprint of Simon & Schuster Children's Publishing Division
1230 Avenue of the Americas, New York, New York 10020
Text and illustrations copyright © 2008 by Anna Walker
First published in Australia in 2008 by Scholastic Press
Published by arrangement with Scholastic Australia Pty Limited
First U.S. edition 2010
All rights reserved, including the right of reproduction in whole
or in part in any form.
SIMON & SCHUSTER BOOKS FOR YOUNG READERS
is a trademark of Simon & Schuster, Inc.
For information about special discounts for bulk purchases,
please contact Simon & Schuster Special Sales at 1-866-506-1949
or business@simonandschuster.com.
The Simon & Schuster Speakers Bureau can bring authors to your live event.
For more information or to book an event, contact the Simon & Schuster
Speakers Bureau at 1-866-248-3049
or visit our website at www.simonspeakers.com.
The text for this book is handwritten by Anna Walker.
The illustrations for this book are rendered in ink on watercolor paper.
Manufactured in Singapore / 0210 TIW
10 9 8 7 6 5 4 3 2 1
CIP data for this book is available from the Library of Congress.
ISBN 978-1-4169-8320-0

I Love Birthdays

by Anna Walker

SIMON & SCHUSTER BOOKS FOR YOUNG READERS
New York • London • Toronto • Sydney

My name is Ollie.

I love birthdays.

I hold my breath

and close my eyes.

My friends give me

a big surprise!

I love treasure hunts,

a yummy treat,

party hats, and dancing feet!

I love green balloons

and party tunes.

I love it when Fred sings,

"Happy Birthday!"

and my friends shout,
"Hip, hip, hooray!"

But what I love best
is to giggle with Fred,
with my birthday balloon
above my bed.